This book belongs to:

. . . .

First published in the UK in 2016 by HarperCollins *Children's Books,*
a division of HarperCollins *Publishers* Ltd, 1 London Bridge Street, London SE1 9GF.
This edition published by HarperCollins *Children's Books* in 2019.

5 7 9 10 8 6 4

ISBN: 978-0-00-797697-3

Based on the script by Lead Writer: Denise Cassar and Team Writers:
Lucy Murphy, Ted Dewan and Mikael Shields. Story by the Bing Writing Team

Adapted from the original books by Ted Dewan and using images created by Acamar Films and Brown Bag Films

Edited by Stella Gurney, Freddie Hutchins and An Vrombaut

Designed by Rachel Lawston

Where's Hoppity?

HarperCollins *Children's Books*

Round the corner, not far away,
Bing takes Hoppity to the park today.

"Hoppity... Voooooosh!"

WAK
WAK

The ducks in the
pond are noisy.

"Flop! That duck
wakked at Hoppity!"

"Perhaps he's saying **hello**," says Flop.

"Yup," giggles Bing.

"Hoppity wants to go to the **playground** now."

"Good idea," says Flop.

"**Let's** go... go... go... **go**...

...Oh! Watch out, Bing!

YUK

"Ooh! Don't step in the dog poo, Flop!"

"Indeed," chuckles Flop.

At the playground, Bing and Hoppity climb
to the top of the slide.

"Oh! I can see Amma from up
here! She's in the garden, Flop!"

wheeeeeeee!

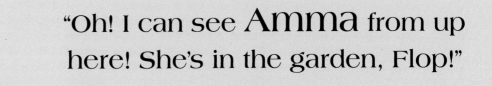

"Hoppity wants to say **hello** to Amma!" says Bing.

"Well then, let's go,"
says Flop.

"But don't
forget the...

uelch!

"...dog poo."

"Flo-o-o-p!"

wails Bing.

"I stepped in the dog pooo!"

Flop helps Bing **hop** over to the bench.

Bing looks at his shoe. "Ooh... it's all **yukky!**"

"Don't worry, Bing – it's no **big thing**. Let's go to Amma's and we'll get you **cleaned up**."

Amma is watering her flowers.

"Amma, I got poo on my shoe!" says Bing.

"Phoo-wee!" says Amma. "We'd better get that washed off."

She cleans Bing's shoe.

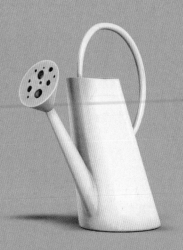

"What were you doing in such a **big hurry** that you didn't see the **doggy poo**, Bing?"

"Me and Hoppity wanted to come and say **hello** to you."

"Oh? Well then, **hello, Bing Bunny.**"

"Hello, Amma," **giggles** Bing. "And you have to say hello to Hoppity…"

Bing doesn't have Hoppity...
and Flop doesn't have him either.

"It's OK, Bing," says Flop. "Hoppity will be
waiting somewhere for you –
we just need to go and find him."

"Ohhh," sniffs Bing. "I waaant Hoppity!"

"Can you **remember** when you last had him?" asks Amma.

Flop picks up a **pinecone** from the path. "Here, Bing – why don't you take this and **pretend** it's Hoppity? It might help you to remember."

"**Good idea,**" says Amma. "What happened first?"

Bing isn't sure.
He **holds** the
pinecone and tries
to remember.

"Erm... the
ducks **wakked**
at Hoppity."

"Good
remembering,
Bing."

"And then we went up the slide
– and we saw you, Amma."

"Then where did
you go?"

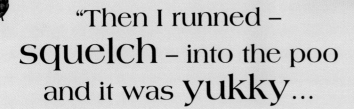

"Then I runned –
squelch – into the poo
and it was yukky...

so we hopped
to the bench..."

"Flop!" gasps Bing.
"I put Hoppity **on the bench!**"

"Then he must be waiting for you **there!**"
Amma smiles. "You'd better go and see!"

But when Bing and Flop arrive
at the bench, Hoppity **isn't** there.

"O**oooohhh**, he's not here, Flop.
I put him on the bench."

"**Hmm**," says Flop.
"I wonder **where** that pinecone is going?"

"It's gone down here," says Bing. And then he spots...

"HOPPITY!"

"Oh, Hoppity!
I found you!"

Bing puts Hoppity to his ear.
"Hoppity says he's glad that
we found him, Flop."

"Good for you,
Bing Bunny."

Hi!

Me and Hoppity played in the park.

The ducks said *wak wak*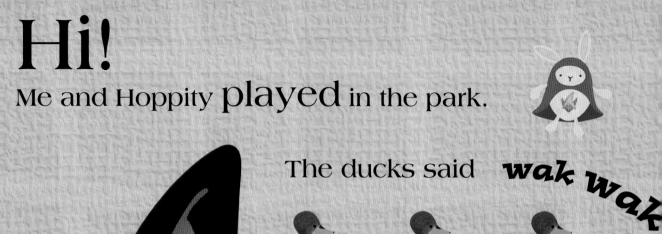

and we went

wheeeeeee

on the slide, but then I standed in POO and Hoppity got lost and I was sad.

So, Flop and Amma gave me a pinecone to help me **remember** all the places we went and that's how I **found** him again.

If you **lose** something, you have to remember **all the things you did** and then you **can find it again.**

Finding Hoppity...

it's a Bing thing.